W9-ATA-520

Angelina's Ballet Class

Story by Katharine Holabird
Based on the illustrations by Helen Craig

Grosset & Dunlap

ISBN 0-448-44013-X   10 9 8 7 6 5 4 3 2 1

Angelina is very excited. She's going
to Miss Lilly's ballet class today. She packs
her pink tutu and two pink slippers in her
ballet bag, and off she goes.

In the dressing room, Angelina meets her
friends. They love ballet class, too. Angelina ties
Alice's ribbons, and Alice fixes Angelina's bow.
In her tutu and slippers, Angelina feels as light
as a feather. She can't wait to start dancing.

"Good morning, Miss Lilly!"
the ballerinas greet their teacher.
Angelina twirls around the dance
studio and then lines up with her
friends.

Miss Quaver sits down and chooses some beautiful piano music to play for the lesson.

Just as the lesson is about to start, Cousin Henry appears, wearing his tiny slippers.

"You can follow Angelina," Miss Lilly says with a smile, and the piano music begins.

"Stretch and bend and touch your toes!" Miss Lilly shows her students how to warm up their muscles with exercises. Angelina can touch her toes quite easily, but Henry still has trouble getting around his tummy!

Angelina stretches her legs
and turns out her feet.
Can you hold very still
like Angelina?

Flora does the splits
and points her toes.
How far can you
stretch your legs?

Alice stretches to the ceiling,
then touches her toes. How
high can you reach?

Alice and Angelina link their hands and
touch their feet. Then they rock back
and forth to stretch their muscles.
Try this with a friend!

Felicity arches her back
and stretches her arms.
Can you bend back
as far as Felicity?

Miss Lilly claps her hands. "Now take your places
at the barre, with backs straight and heads up."
Angelina and her friends hold the barre tightly
and lift their legs higher and higher, until they can
do beautiful arabesques just like Miss Lilly.

Henry tries to copy Angelina as she checks her position in the mirror, but he can't quite reach the barre!

All the dancers practice ballet positions together.

"First, second, third, fourth, fifth," repeats Miss Lilly. Angelina holds her arms above her head and balances in fifth position.

"Very good," Miss Lilly encourages everyone.

Henry gets confused, so Angelina helps him to cross his feet and stand very still.

First Position

Second Position

Third Position

Fourth Position

Fifth Position

"Now we'll take turns practicing leaps," Miss Lilly says with a smile.

Angelina is first in line. She loves to leap as high as she can—she feels as if she's flying across the room.

All the other dancers take their turns. Henry runs to keep up with them, then does his own funny jump.

"Bravo," Miss Lilly applauds.

"Point your toes and pirouette," Miss Lilly says. The ballerinas follow her as she spins gracefully around the room.

Angelina starts to twirl very fast and accidentally bumps into Alice.

Henry gets so dizzy, he has to sit down for a minute. Sometimes pirouettes can be difficult!

Miss Lilly is very pleased with her ballet students. "Soon we'll give a recital for all the parents," she announces proudly.

Angelina and Alice are going to be the Sunflower Princesses. They try on their flower costumes and dance in front of the mirrors. Henry buzzes after them, pretending to be a busy bee.

Felicity does a sideways leap called a
pas de chat (pah de SHAH).
Pas de chat means "cat step."
Can you step like a cat, too?

Alice can do a lovely arabesque
(ar-uh-BESK). She balances on tiptoe
and lifts one leg straight behind her. If
you stand on tiptoe, you can
do an arabesque, too.

Angelina practices a grand jeté
(gron juh-TAY). She loves to
leap very high with her legs
outstretched in the air. Can you
leap as high as Angelina?

Flora does a graceful pirouette
(peer-uh-WET). When she spins
in a circle, she holds her head still.
Can you pirouette like Flora?

Henry practices a plié (plee-AY).
He bends his knees lower and
lower and tries not to wobble.
Try to bend way down like
Henry, but don't wobble!

"All together now, listen to the music as we dance," Miss Lilly says.

She helps Angelina and her friends rehearse the movements for the *Sunflower Ballet* until they know every step by heart.

Henry can't remember his steps, so Angelina helps him by dancing like a bee, too.

When class is over, Angelina and the other ballerinas perform a révérence (ray-vay-RAHNS). This is a way to say thank you and good-bye to Miss Lilly.

Angelina does an elegant curtsy, and Henry does a formal bow. "Good-bye, Miss Lilly."

Miss Lilly waves to everyone. "See you next week!"

Angelina smiles. She can hardly wait to dance again with her friends at Miss Lilly's Ballet School.

See Angelina Dance!

1. Remove the two twelve-inch pieces of ribbon from the front of the book.

2. Remove the punch-out pages from the back of the book. Tear apart each flip-book page.

3. Arrange the flip-book pages in order, from 1 to 48. Tap the stack of pages against a hard surface so that the holes align.

4. Thread the ribbons through the holes. Tie them tightly.

5. Bend the pages down with your thumb. Let the pages flip up—you'll see Angelina dance!